for Jessica,
Aurèlie and Magali
with love

V.F.

for Christopher
with love

C.S.

SIMON & SCHUSTER BOOKS FOR YOUNG READERS
Simon & Schuster Building, Rockefeller Center,
1230 Avenue of the Americas,
New York, New York 10020
Text copyright © 1991 by Vivian French
Illustrations copyright © 1991 by Clive Scruton
All rights reserved including the
right of reproduction in whole or in
part in any form.
First U.S. Edition 1992
Originally published in Great Britain
by Walker Books Limited.
SIMON & SCHUSTER BOOKS FOR YOUNG READERS
is a trademark of Simon & Schuster.

Manufactured in Hong Kong.

10 9 8 7 6 5 4 3 2 1

Library of Congress Cataloging-in-Publication Data
French, Vivian.
    It's a go to the park day / by Vivian French ;
illustrated by Clive Scruton.
        p.   cm.
    Summary: When everyone refuses to take Milo
the mole to the park, he goes by himself, leaving a
trail for the others to follow.
    [1. Moles (Animals)—Fiction.   2. Parks—Fiction.]   I. Scruton.
Clive, ill.   II. Title.
PZ7.F88917It   1992
[E]—dc20   90-28506   CIP
ISBN: 0-671-74477-1

It's a Go-to-the-Park Day

Written by
Vivian **F**rench

Illustrated by
Clive **S**cruton

SIMON & SCHUSTER BOOKS
FOR YOUNG READERS

Published by Simon & Schuster
New York · London · Toronto · Sydney · Tokyo · Singapore

It was very early in the morning.
Milo the mole opened the window, rubbed
his eyes, and smiled. "Hooray!" he said and
bounced off the bed.

"GRAN!" shouted Milo. "GRAN!
It's a go-to-the-park day, and I think
we need to go now!"

"But Milo dear,
it's much too early,"
said Gran.

"Rats!" said Milo.

"Millie!" Milo burst through the door.
"Millie! I want you to take me to the park!"
"NO," said Millie. "GO AWAY!"
"Rats!" said Milo.

"Hello, Spencer," said Milo. "I'm up."
"So am I," said Spencer. "And I'm busy."
"Wouldn't you like to come to the park with me?" Milo asked.
"No chance," said Spencer.
"Rats," said Milo.

 Milo dressed and went
down to the kitchen.

"If I went to the swings today,"
he said thoughtfully, "I bet I
could swing all by myself. And I could climb
up the monkey bars right to the top."
Milo helped himself to a cookie.
"And I *do* know the way to the park...."

He sat very still.

"But I'm not allowed to play
outside on my own. But
I won't be playing, will I?
I'll be going somewhere.
So it'll be all right."
Milo got the shopping
cart. "I need to pack
for the park," he said.

He looked in the cupboards.
"String's useful. I'll take that.
And clothes pins.
Cookies and apples.
And my sweater
and a hankie,
so Gran won't
be angry."

Milo was halfway along the road when he stopped. "I wonder if I'll know my house when I come home?" he said.
He trotted back and carefully pinned his hankie to the gate. "Now I'll know," he said.

Milo reached the corner of the road. "And I'll tie my sweater to the bridge to show me the way home."

There was a great
deal of string left over.
"I'll make a trail,"
Milo decided.
    The string was very long
    and it reached all the way to the park

Milo tied the string to the bottom of the monkey bars and began to climb.

"I'm at the top! I'm at the top!" he shouted.

But there was nobody there to hear.

Milo ate his cookies.

Then he went on the swings.

"Look at me—look at me—I'm almost swinging!" he called.

But no one said, "Oh Milo, well done!"

He had a turn on the slide, but there was
no one to say "WHEEEEE!" as he flew down to
the ground.

Milo sat on the merry-go-round. It stayed
quite still. "Rats," said Milo.

He ate his apples. "Oh dear," Milo said.
"I do wish Gran was here."

Back at home, Gran was looking for Milo.
"Spencer dear, is Milo here with you?"
"He's been eating cookies,"
Spencer said, looking in the jar.
Millie peered out of the window.
"There's something on
the gate," she said.
They hurried into
the yard.

"Gran," Spencer said, "it's Milo's hankie."

"OH! OH! OH!" Millie jumped up and down. "Milo's run away! Because I was mean to him."

"You're *always* mean to him," said Spencer.

"But I told him to GO AWAY!" Millie said, beginning to cry.

"My poor little Milo," said Gran, "we must find him."

Spencer rode his scooter down the road and asked the mailman if he had seen Milo. "No," said the mailman.

Millie ran down the road the other way and asked the roadsweeper if she had seen Milo. "No," said the roadsweeper.

Gran stopped the papergirl and asked her if she had seen Milo. "I think I saw his sweater on the bridge," said the papergirl.

Gran, Millie, Spencer, the mailman, the
roadsweeper and the papergirl all rushed
down the road to the bridge.

"Look!" said Spencer, ringing his bell wildly.
"Follow the string!"

"MILO!" shouted Gran, Millie, Spencer, the mailman, the roadsweeper and the papergirl.

Milo sat up.

"Oh, Milo dear," said Gran, "we were so worried— but we've all come to take you safely home."

Milo burst into tears.

"What is it?" Millie asked. "Have you got a pain?"

Waaaa!!!

"It's not fair," Milo sobbed. "I asked and asked you to take me to the park and now that you've come, you just want to take me home again!"

Gran wiped his nose
and sighed. "Well, now that
we are here, I suppose
we can stay for a while."
"Hooray!" cried Milo, giving Gran a hug.

"Will you push me
on the swings?

And watch me on
the monkey bars?

And push me on
the merry-go-round?
And see me whizz
down the slide?"

Gran nodded. "Yes, dear."

"I just knew it was a go-to-the-park day,"
said Milo.